Text copyright © 1995 by Stephen Wyllie
Illustrations copyright © 1995 by Ken Brown
All rights reserved.
CIP Data is available.
Published in the United States 1996 by
Dutton Children's Books,
a division of Penguin Books USA Inc.
375 Hudson Street, New York, New York 10014
Originally published in Great Britain 1995 by
Andersen Press Ltd., London
Typography by Julia Goodman
Printed in Italy
First American Edition
ISBN 0-525-45648-1
1 3 5 7 9 10 8 6 4 2

A FLEA IN THE EAR

by Stephen Wyllie ❖ illustrated by Ken Brown

DUTTON CHILDREN'S BOOKS • New York

One moonlit night, as the spotted dog was making sure his hens were all tucked into bed, he heard a twig snap in the woods nearby. "I know you're out there, fox!" he barked. "Stay away from my hens."

"Good evening," said the wily fox politely as he sauntered into the farmyard.

"Back off," said the dog, "or I'll bite."

"I wouldn't dream of taking one of your scrawny hens," lied the fox. "I much prefer a nice, fat, juicy duck."

"All right," said the dog, scratching his fleas. "Just remember
what I said."

"I will," said the fox. "I see you have some flea trouble."

"Don't talk about it," said the dog. "At this time of year, it's
agony."

"I never have any trouble myself," said the fox. "But then, I know the secret that keeps them away."

"You do?" asked the dog eagerly. "Please tell me."

"I couldn't possibly," the fox replied. "It's an old family secret, handed down from father to son for generations."

"Oh, please tell," pleaded the dog. "I'd give anything to get rid of my fleas."

"Anything?" asked the fox slyly. "I suppose I could tell you—in exchange for five or six of your stringy birds."

"Definitely not," said the dog indignantly. "I'd lose my job."
"Oh, well," said the fox, "suit yourself. Bye-bye."
And he left the unhappy dog to scratch away for the rest of the
night.

Late the following day, the fox came back.

"Good evening," he said. "I've been thinking things over and have decided to tell you the secret for free. I couldn't allow a fellow creature to suffer so much pain."

"That's wonderful," said the dog. "What's the secret?"

"It's quite simple, really. You just trot over the hill, down the other side, through the gate, and along the lane until you come to a pond. Wade into the water, and, as it gets deeper, the fleas will climb up your legs. Soon only your head will be dry, and all the fleas will be on it. If you take a deep breath and dunk your head under the water, all your fleas will drown."

"Great!" cried the dog. "I'm surprised I never thought of it myself."

"While you're gone," said the fox, "I'll watch the chickens. Just think, you'll be flea-free for the first time in your life."

"I can hardly wait," yelped the dog, and he galloped off up the hill, down to the gate, and along to the pond to drown his fleas.

As he lowered himself into the water, he was amazed to hear a voice in his ear.

"I know you are about to drown us," said a flea, "but if you spare our lives, we will all jump off and promise never to bite you again."

The dog paused for a moment.

"Oh, all right. But you have to promise."

He waded back to the edge of the pond, and all the fleas leaped off.
The happy dog went home. But when he got back, he found that the
fox had vanished. He soon discovered that all his hens were gone, too.

"Oh, no!" howled the dog. "I'll lose my job! I'll be homeless!"
He flopped down in despair. Suddenly, he noticed a trail of
feathers leading into the woods.

He got up and followed the trail until he came to the fox's den.
He pawed politely at the door. The fox opened it.

"Hello," said the fox, acting surprised. "What brings you here?"

"I just dropped by to tell you," said the dog, pretending to
scratch, "I went for your flea cure but couldn't get into the pond.

"It was full to the brim with fat, juicy ducks."

"It was?" asked the fox, licking his lips.

"Overflowing," lied the dog. "I'll try again later when they have gone. Bye-bye."

"Good-bye," said the fox, and closed the door.

The dog hid behind a tree. He didn't have to wait long before
the fox came out of his den with an empty sack over his shoulder.
After a quick look around, he slipped off toward the pond.

But when he got there, he didn't see a trace of the fat, juicy ducks the dog had talked about. While the fox stared at the pond in disbelief, all the fleas that had nearly drowned hopped joyfully onto his furry back.

Meanwhile, the dog had broken down the fox's door, and there, sure enough, he found a squawking bagful of his hens. He gathered them up gently and took them back to their coop, determined never to let them out of his sight again.